AF472776

Kahraman

The Bare Feet Belly Dancer

Rima Ibara

authorHOUSE®

AuthorHouse™ UK Ltd.
500 Avebury Boulevard
Central Milton Keynes, MK9 2BE
www.authorhouse.co.uk
Phone: 08001974150

First published by AuthorHouse 11/10/2009

ISBN: 978-1-4490-3310-1 (sc)

This book is printed on acid-free paper.

About The Author

Born on the 20th of August 1979, of a Jordanian origin, Rima Jbara was known as the youngest author in The Middle East to write her first novel at the age of fourteen in a second language to her. Today, she has a total of thirteen books, with a Bachelor Degree in English Literature and Communication & Masters Degree in Strategic Marketing.

To know more information about Rima log onto the author's websites www.rima-jbara.com

ꕥ

"I had a lot of toys when I was a child, but I never liked to play with any of them."

ꕥ

"When I was very young, I remembered her crying in the night, when she thought I was asleep. I watched her in silence. Then I wondered who the person she cried for was. When I grew up, I knew. It was my father. Later, I cried too."

ꕥ

"As a child, my body moved gently, like a leaf hit by the air."

ꕥ

"My grandmother would dye her single pair of shoes white in summer and black in winter, just to be able to afford to buy me a new pair of shoes. I would say to her, 'Dada when I grow up I'll buy you a lot of shoes.' And I did."

ꕥ

"When we had our break in school, I did not sit with the other girls to chat. I was busy thinking about many other things."

ঞ

"I had many beautiful dresses. Dada would sew me a new dress every three weeks. Girls at school would stare at my clothes – not knowing how Dada suffered and did not sleep at night, just to get the money for the expensive materials she used."

ঞ

"I never felt poor for one second."

ঞ

"I remember her working all night, sewing endlessly. For all the rich women she knew, to earn money and to survive. She looked very exhausted. She never complained. She always smiled. I always felt her love. I made a vow. I would repay her for all the lost nights and I would never let her work again."

ঞ

"Dada would cook fish every day for lunch, though it was very expensive. She wanted me to be well nourished."

ঞ

"I will never show my grief to the people."

ঞ

"How did my mother die?"
"While giving birth to you."

"I wish I knew her."
"She would have been a wonderful mother."
"Thank you for giving me her photograph."
"That's the only one I have."
"I thank God every day for having you Dada."
"I love you very much."
"I don't know what would happen to me without you?"

ଓ

"Did my father suffer when he died?"
"Yes he did."
"I wish I was able to take all the pain from his body and put it into my body."
"No dear, you are very young and you have a long life ahead of you to live.
"I thank God every day for having you Dada."
"God protect you."

ଓ

"Is there anything in common between me and my mother's personality?"
"Both of you have strong personalities."
"Did my mother work?"
"No, but she took good care of your father."

ଓ

"Is there anything in common between me and my father's personality?"
"Both of you are stubborn."
"What did my father work as?"
"He was a geology teacher."

ꟲ

"Who named me Kahraman?"
"You're father."
"I never heard of any girl in my school with such a name."
"I remember him telling me that it is the name of a valuable gem."

ꟲ

"How I wish my parents were still alive. All my life would have been different."

ꟲ

"The house I live in may not have expensive furniture. But it has something more important to me and that is my father's and mother's touch."

ꟲ

"I want to move my body not to rhythms of music but according to the events of my life."

ꟲ

"I do not know why people like to criticize me? Why can't they accept me as I am?"

ꟲ

"I know that I'm not well-educated. But that doesn't mean that I'm ignorant."

ꟲ

"Why do they judge my character in a negative way, just because I work in something they cannot accept?"

ꟹ

"Who are you to judge me? You are a human being like me. What gives you the right to do so?"

ꟹ

"I am important to some people and nothing to others."

ꟹ

"I want people to forget everything when they see me. And remember only happiness."

ꟹ

"I want to puzzle the world. Never let them know which piece goes with which piece. Make all the pieces similar to one another. And laugh at their confusion."

ꟹ

"Are you sure about what you're going to do with your life?"
"Yes."
"Think twice before taking the first step."
"I already did."
"They are going to tear you apart with their hurtful comments."
"Do not worry Dada."
"Please take care of yourself."
"I will."

ꟹ

"People talked. People pointed their fingers towards me, when I chose a career that was disrespected in our culture. I ignored them, because I believed that what I did was an art, which gave me the chance to be creative. I insisted on what I was doing, so I held my head up high, knowing that I would succeed one day."

೧૩

"I stood behind the door listening as Lady Azhar shouted at Dada. She was complaining how her work was becoming worse with the passing days. I could not wait any longer. I had to put an end to this situation. And fast."

೧૩

"No one knows how much I wanted a baby to live and breathe inside of me."
"Do not express it to anyone."
"I cannot."
"Do not let anyone feel sorry for you."
"And then what?"
"Nobody's perfect."
"Did I ask for it?"

೧૩

"Women, it is time to rise. Let us show them what we are capable of doing. And I will lead the way for all of you."

೧૩

"I'm a feminist. And what is wrong with that?"

೧૩

"It is time to give value to the women's world."

ℭℨ

"In my opinion, traditions are made to be changed. And I will change every one of them."

ℭℨ

"I want to do what no other woman has dared to do in her time."

ℭℨ

Kahraman did not sleep for days. She tried to. But it was of no use. She lost her appetite for food. She would force herself to eat. But it was a hopeless case. She lost weight. She was very thin. She was pale. She looked sick. The healthy Kahraman no longer existed. It had been weeks since she looked at herself in the mirror. She refused to work. She did not want to do anything. All she did was cry.

"What am I living for? I do not have the most important thing in the life of a woman. I have other things, but why not this one? I want this one. I'm not asking for more. I will never ask for more, if I could only have it. Why me? What luck I have? Now, what am I to do? Accept that horrible fact just like that? It seems so. But I cannot. I feel that I'm dying and slowly."

Hanan would sit in the house all the time, refusing to leave, in case something happened to Kahraman. She was heartbroken for her granddaughter. She did not want to see her suffering. She wanted to help her. She could no longer bare her cries and not say a word.
"Please my love. Stop crying. Dry your tears. They cannot help you."
"What do you want me to do?"
"I know it is hard. But you have to accept that fact."

"I cannot."
"Yes, you can. You cannot do anything about it."
"If only I could."
"Kahraman, God gave you almost everything."

ꟹ

"But I wanted this one."
"You cannot have everything you want in life."
"I did not ask for everything."
"Nobody's perfect."
"All I wanted is this…" and she burst into tears.
"Go, stand in front of the mirror. See yourself. You look like a ghost. You are sinking, and very deep. I can still help you now. But later on, it will be too late. Think. Fast. There is not much time left. For how long has it been like that?"
"I do not remember."
"Do you want me to remind you?"
"No."
"You went a long way, Kahraman. You fought for yourself. Do not stop now. Or else everything will be gone for nothing. You must continue with what you did. You cannot back off now."
"Does it matter?"
"Where is my strong Kahraman? Where did she go?"

Hanan was sick of the dark room. She opened the curtains. Light filled the room that had been dark for months. Kahraman closed her eyes, unable to bear the light. She had got used to the darkness. Then, Hanan pulled her granddaughter towards the mirror. Kahraman looked at the unknown image in the mirror. That was not her. She could not believe how much she had changed.

"What do you see?"
There was no reply.

ꟹ

Egypt 1950

Kahraman wore a red dress that had been finished this morning by Hanan. They both selected the design from a fashion catalogue. Kahraman matched the dress with silver sandals, and brushed her long brown hair then stood in front of the mirror for one final look. Her slim figure looked perfect in the red dress. There was a smile of satisfaction on her face.

Hanan was sleeping. Kahraman did not want to wake her up. So she left. It was evening. And the roads were filled with people. She took a taxi and on the way, many thoughts were rising in her mind.

"I dance very well. I have been practicing for months. There is no excuse for failure. I must dance in that club because it is the best in Cairo. I need the money since I told Dada to stop working. I must get the money, or else, there won't be food on the table."

Kahraman arrived and stood in front of the huge building, staring at the board that was placed on the head of the building. "Salma Club". It was the name of the founder and owner of the club.

"One day, I will have my own club with my name on it," Kahraman said with persistence. She walked in and looked around. She was astounded by the rich furniture that was used. She kept on walking until she found a man sitting behind a desk.
"Good evening, may I see Salma?"
"Why do you want to see her?"
"I want to work here."
"Wait."

The man stared at Kahraman, from head to toe, before he made a move to the door. The man entered an office. Minutes passed and he still did not come out. Kahraman wondered what could have delayed him so much. After several minutes, he came out. He waved for her and she walked into a room.

"Go straight, then right," the man directed.

Kahraman followed his instructions and reached a noisy room. The room was filled with women, some sitting, some standing, some good looking, some bad looking, and most of them chatting to one another. For a second, everyone was silent and stared at her. She walked to stand in a corner.

"Are all these women waiting for the same reason as I am?" she wondered. The door opened and a man came out. He stood in the middle of the room and looked around. His gaze moved from one girl to another and finally stopped at Kahraman.

"You, with the very long brown hair, follow me," he ordered. Envious eyes riveted on Kahraman.

She followed the man into the office to find another man standing next to the office.

"What's your name, pretty face?"

"Kahraman."

"I want your real name?"

"It is my real name."

"Do you want to sing or dance?"

"I want to dance."

"Okay, go to that room, on the left."

Kahraman moved to where he pointed and entered the room. She saw a woman sitting behind a desk, surrounded by men and women. One of the men approached her, "Who told you to enter here?"

"I'm sorry; they told me to enter this room."

"Maybe it was Ahmad," he said.

"I do not know."

"Let the girl come closer," the woman said.
Kahraman moved closer and stood in front of the woman.
"Do you want to sing or dance?" Salma asked, as her gaze moved over Kahraman's body.
"I want to dance."
"You are one pretty girl, but can you dance?"
"Yes, I have been practicing for months."
"You mean you never worked anywhere before?" Salma asked, with a frown.
"This would be my first."
"Go, choose a record from there, play it and dance. Show me how good you are."

Kahraman selected one of the records and played it. She walked to the centre of the room and started to move her body. Everybody was silent and stared at her. After several minutes, the record finished and Kahraman stood in front of Salma, anxious to know what she would say.

"Not bad. But you need more practice and especially under someone professional," the woman said.
"Am I accepted?"
"Yes. Be here tomorrow at four. You will practice every day with Nada as much as she thinks you need to. Then the tailor will take your size to prepare costumes. You will start dancing with a group of girls. You will earn a little in the beginning. After that we will see what happens."
Kahraman nodded as Salma continued talking, "What is your name?"
"Kahraman."
"I want your real name!"
"It is my real name."
"I wanted to give you a stage name but I see you have a nice name that does not need to be changed. How old are you?"
"I am seventeen."

"Too young, but that is not a problem. I will see you tomorrow."
Happiness filled Kahraman's heart as she rushed home to tell Hanan the good news.

"Dada, I made it."
"I knew you would. Congratulations. Tell me all about it."
Hanan and Kahraman sat together as they ate. Their chat lasted till late into the night. Next morning, Kahraman woke up late.
"Why did you not wake me up earlier?"
"I wanted you to sleep more, my love."
Kahraman smiled as she sat, eating her breakfast.
"I will have to go and prepare myself for practice."
"I want you to take care of yourself. And God protect you."
"Thank you, Dada."

Kahraman waited in the practice room for Nada.
"Are you Kahraman?"
"Yes."
Nada eyed her pupil carefully.
"I want you to dance on that song."

Kahraman danced to the rhythms of the music as best as she could, as Nada sat watching her dancing. She did dance very well. In Nada's eyes, Kahraman was the first beautiful young dancer she was ever going to train. But Kahraman could do better. And Nada wanted to help her. There was some star quality in Kahraman that Salma and Nada realized. Kahraman trained for hours until Nada told her to stop. Both were exhausted. Kahraman did not have the chance to make friends with any of the girls around her. She was busy learning and listening to Nada's instructions. Kahraman then went to Salma's office.

"It's good you passed by my office. I wanted to talk to you. How is the training?"

"The training is very interesting. I'm learning a lot. Nada is helping me in every way she can."
"Good. You have to show up here at eleven for the show. It finishes at twelve. Do you want to sit with the customers?"
"No."
"Then go to the tailor, let him fix something for you. You must have a costume by tonight."
Kahraman left to go to the tailor while Nada went to Salma's office.
"You wanted me?"
"Yes, Nada come in. How is Kahraman?"
"Extremely good, she has her own style. With some training she will be perfect."
"Is she taking it seriously?"
"Yes, she is."
"Take care of her. She is different. She might be our new star."
"It has been a long time since we got anyone with star quality. Do not worry Salma."
"I want her ready within weeks. She will be dancing solo."

Kahraman wore her costume that fitted her properly then applied light make up and finally brushed her long light brown hair. She was ready. She never took much time to prepare herself. She stood with the girls, waiting for the curtains to open. She could not wait till the curtains opened. She was anxious to see the audience. Kahraman heard the girls next to her talking about their fears. She smiled with confidence and took a deep breath. The music started. The curtains opened. And Kahraman started dancing to the rhythms of the music. She found a huge audience staring at her. She smiled and relaxed. Salma and Nada sat watching the show. Salma smiled. She was pleased by what she saw.

"She dances in a classy way. Do you think she will make it Salma?"

"She will. I know it when I see a star."
"Why is her costume different?"
"I made her wear a different costume so that the audience would notice her."
"I think you are helping her very much."
"We will see if she deserves it."

When Kahraman arrived at the main entrance of the building she heard two women chatting each from her their balcony.
"Look, Ilham, at which time she is returning home!" said one of the women.
"I know. She does not know how to earn money in a better way," replied the other woman.
"I wonder what she is doing!"
"Who knows?"
Kahraman ignored what she heard and walked straight to her apartment. She entered to find Hanan still awake.
"Dada, why are you still awake?"
"I was worried about you. I could not sleep without you being in the house."
"Here I am. Now, go to sleep."
"Do you want to eat?"
"I'm too tired to eat."
"Tell me, how did it go?"
"The costume was okay. I wore black, while the rest of the girls wore pink."
"Oh! That distinguishes you from the others."
"I know. There were a lot of people."
"How is the place?"
"Dada, come with me tomorrow and see."
"I will not bother you?"
"No you won't Dada."
"I will."

Hanan sat watching Kahraman practicing bare feet and she was getting tired but refused to stop. She followed all of Nada's instructions. After the hours passed, Kahraman sat next to Hanan.

"We have finished for today. I'm thirsty."
Kahraman drank water then asked, "Am I good Dada?"
"I did not know that you were that good. You dance like a butterfly."
"That is the nicest thing I have ever heard."
"Is your schedule like this every day?"
"Yes. Why?"
"It is hard work."
"Do not worry about me, Dada. Let us go home. I need a shower. And some sleep."

All the girls who worked in the club noticed the beautiful Kahraman. But today she was not alone. Hanan went to see the place. She loved the furniture and design of the club. Hanan sat talking to Nada while Kahraman wore her costume.
"Thank you for taking care of Kahraman."
"She has a talent. And I want to nurture it."
"Do you think that she is good?"
"Yes. She will be better after some time."

Hanan smiled as Kahraman called her. Hanan entered the dressing room that was crowded with girls. They all whispered and giggled. Until one of them said, "Look girls, she has brought a chaperon with her."

Kahraman and Hanan ignored them. Hanan brushed Kahraman's long brown hair as she applied a brush of make up. Many girls envied Kahraman. Hanan saw it in their eyes when they stared at her granddaughter. Hanan looked at the atmosphere surrounding Kahraman. The girls behaved cheaply. They were talking about the men they went out with. Her granddaughter pretended not to listen to their talk, while Hanan was getting worried. She did not want Kahraman to be like one of them.

Hanan watched from backstage the huge crowd. They all looked handsomely rich with high positions in life and her lovely butterfly dancing in the middle of many girls.

"My love, I'm worried about you."
"Why?"
"The atmosphere is very filthy."
"This is the best club in the country. So things are better than other places."
Hanan did not say a word.
"Dada, I have grown up. I'm no longer a child. I can take care of myself."
"God protect you."

Kahraman's schedule was the same every day for months. She was improving in her dancing. She obeyed Nada completely. She listened carefully every time Salma told her something. She never interfered with anybody's work. She never complained about anything. She never asked for more money. She was content for the time being. She maintained a high position in the eyes of the people who worked with her.

"My love, why are you up so early?"
"I want to take you shopping."
"I do not want anything."
"Do not argue, Dada. Get dressed."
Kahraman brought Hanan a lot of things especially shoes. Kahraman had once made a promise when she was a child and she kept it.

"Kahraman, I want to talk to you now."
"Excuse me, Nada. I'll be back soon."
Kahraman followed Salma to her office.
"From now on you will be dancing alone."
"What happened?"
"You're very good now. Do you not like to dance alone?"
"Yes. Of course I want to."
"The program will be changed next week. I will start advertising from now about your solo dance. I want you to practice hard. The tailor will arrive today at seven to bring you several costumes for your dances. Check them before leaving."
Kahraman smiled and asked, "Anything more?"
"Ah! Tomorrow you must be here at twelve for the photo shoot. I need to have pictures of you for the advertisement."
"I will be here."

Kahraman was thrilled. She knew that there was a lot of work to be done. Her solo dance meant more practice. And most vital of all, she needed to work on the photo shoot. She had never posed before. That meant she had to work on it today. Kahraman continued with her rehearsal. It was late when she finished. Then she tried on her costumes. They fitted her properly. But she hated the colours. They were brown with grey, and thought, "When I become famous, I will choose the designs and colors myself."

"Dada, I will rehearse in my room for a while."
"You have already practiced."
"This time it is for how to pose in front of the mirror."
"Why?"
"I have a photo shoot tomorrow morning."
"Good. You will have pictures of your own."

Kahraman took a shower. She prepared herself for the show. Then she sat in front of the mirror. She tried several poses. She studied her postures. And she checked which angles would be photogenic. Hanan watched Kahraman from behind the door and thought; "She will be something in the future. What she is doing now is unusual." After two hours Hanan called her, "My love, come to dinner."

"What did you learn about?"

"I learned several matters Dada."

"Like what?"

"My nose is a bit long, compared to my slim face, so it would look obvious if I pose in a profile style."

"I have not noticed that."

"Also, my smile is a bit wide. My gums show, which means I should lower my smile down."

"Do not be picky. You are beautiful, as you are."

"I know I am, but I can be more beautiful if I know how to correct the expressions in my face."

Kahraman ate her dinner, but Hanan was not pleased.

"You eat very small portions."

"I'm full. I cannot eat more."

"I will take you to a doctor. You will become thinner. You are already thin."

"Well, that is how God created me."

"If you eat more, then you will become fatter."

"I like the way I am now."

Hanan knew how stubborn her granddaughter was. It was impossible to convince her. But she would try to stuff her with food from time to time.

"Dada, I'm going. Wish me luck. It is my first solo dance."

"Good luck. And God protect you."

"Sleep well, Dada."

"I will not, until you come back."

"See. I'm not the only stubborn one around here."

Now Kahraman had her own dressing room. She felt a relief. She would not have to be with the other girls who kept staring at her. She prepared herself carefully. Salma and Nada sat in the booth, waiting for Kahraman to come up on stage. It was time. Kahraman stood behind the curtains. Within seconds, the music started. The curtains opened. As the lovely butterfly moved her body.

"Wait for a month and see what Kahraman will be," Salma said to Nada.
"I know."
"She is beautiful. She is a superb dancer. She has quality on stage. And most important of all is that when she emerges on stage most of the people are not able to remove their eyes from her." Salma stood to go see the customers.
"Salma, how are you tonight?"
"Optimistic."
"You look nice."
"Thank you."
"I see there is a change in the program."
"Yes, we have a new dancer."
"She is excellent."

Salma was pleased to hear that one of her most important customers had said so. But it was not only him. Many other customers said the same thing. But Kahraman never stayed to hear the comments of her audience. As she walked to her apartment, someone threw water at her from the top of the building. She did not bother to see who it was. She continued walking to her apartment.

"Hello, Dada."
"You are wet."
"Someone threw water on me."
"It must be one of the neighbors. I warned you about the reaction of people."
"They think they bothered me. Well, they did not."

"Go, take a shower. And come tell me about your solo dance."

Next day, Kahraman applied red lipstick then added some false lashes. She brushed her long silky brown hair, and wore her red dress and stood in front of the camera.
"It was time to flirt with the camera," she thought.
"I want to take pictures of you in normal clothes and in your costume."

Kahraman nodded as she started to pose. She remembered what she had learned yesterday. The photographer did not have to direct her. She knew how to move the way he wanted her to. They finished after sometime. Kahraman went for training. The dancer was getting tired yet, she never complained. She liked what she did. Kahraman slept soundly as Hanan watched her.
"Please, God protect her from the envious eyes of people. Keep her in good health. And keep her happy."

The weeks passed by and Kahraman was the rising star of the club. The club was earning more money than it ever did. Kahraman had a loyal audience that came especially to see her. She received many flowers, with invitations from rich and important men. She kept the flowers, but threw out the cards. She never bothered to even read them. Kahraman locked her dressing room so no one could enter to see her. After the performance, she would clean her face from the make-up, tie her hair, and wear a black coat to leave. The driver of the club would take her back home.

The rising star would sit late into the night, looking at her pictures. She studied them carefully learning from her mistakes. She realized what poses suited her and what did not suit her.

"My dear, we should go buy some materials. You do not have many clothes."

"No, you will not sew anything for me from now on. It is time for you to rest. I will go and buy some clothes."
"I want to come with you."

Kahraman and her grandmother went shopping for hours. Kahraman picked the colors she liked. She searched for things that were unique and elegant. There were several photographers from many magazines who came to the club to take pictures of its latest star. Kahraman smiled and posed for them.

ଓଃ

"People have a stereotype image of a belly dancer that is completely wrong."

ଓଃ

"The beginning is always the easiest. The problems begin once you reach the top, which is where the difficulty is, because you have to live up to expectations."

ଓଃ

"I'm proud to climb the ladder step by step."

ଓଃ

"I do not want to be just any dancer, but a trademark in the world of dancers."

ଓଃ

"There is a certain red line a belly dancer should not trespass when making her costume, otherwise, she would be considered something else."

ଓ

Kahraman took a shower after working out and sat with Hanan.
"Dada, my parents are constantly on my mind at night."
"If they were alive, then things would have been different."
"I wonder what would have happened."
"You would be in university by now."
"How do you know?"
"Your father wanted you to be a doctor."
"I like doctors. But I do not like to be one of them."
"They would have objected to your career."
"Do you think so?"
"I'm sure your father would not like it."
"Maybe, but I like it very much."

"May I see Salma?" the man asked.
"You're name?"
"Salem, she knows me."
Within seconds, Salma was out.
"It has been a long time, how are you?"
"Well. And you?"
"As you can see, kindly come into my office."
"How is the club doing?"
"Doing fine; and what about your film production?"
"In the process, I would like to know more about Kahraman."
"Ask me and I will answer all your questions."
"I'm doing a movie with Waheed and he is looking for a dancer."
"Can you and Waheed come tonight to see Kahraman dance?"
"Yes, but do not tell her anything, till we decide."
"See you tonight."

"She is thin. But there is nothing wrong in her body physically," the doctor said.

"Is she healthy?"
"Yes."
"But she does not eat well, doctor."
"Yes, I do," Kahraman interrupted.
"Nothing is wrong with her," the doctor assured Hanan.

Waheed and Salem sat in the front. The unaware Kahraman prepared herself beautifully and was dancing happily.
"She is very pretty, but can she act?" Salem whispered to Waheed.
"I'm sure she can. She is the dancer I'm looking for."

The next day, while Kahraman was practicing, Salem came in to watch her. After an hour he approached her.
"Kahraman, my name is Salem."
"Pleased to meet you Sir, what can I do for you?"
"I'm a producer. I'm doing a movie with the singer Waheed. And we need a dancer. Are you interested?"
Without any thought, Kahraman replied, "Yes, very much."
"Finish your preparation and come to Salma's office. I will be waiting there for you."

Kahraman knocked the door and heard Salma saying, "Come in".
"Oh! Kahraman you have finished at last."
"I'm sorry for keeping you waiting."
"It is okay," Salem said with a smile.
"Kahraman, do you want to act in Waheed's movie?"
"Yes."
"Then, in this case, you will have to stop dancing in the club till you finish the movie."
"When am I supposed to start?"
"Today, you will take the script to know your lines. Also, you have to meet Waheed in the evening to discuss the dancing scenes."

"Should I come to the studio now to pick the script?"
"That would be a good idea. Better than waiting till tomorrow to send it to you. In this way we will not waste time. You will find Waheed there practicing. So you can sit and discuss things.
"Today, I will announce to your audience that tonight is to be your last dance till you're movie is finished in production." Salma added.
Kahraman excused herself and rushed to change her clothes, shower and prepare herself so she could go with Salem right away.
"I expected you to take more time."
"You have waited enough."
"I wish all women were like that."
Salem and Kahraman rode in his fancy car and went to the studio. She loved the place. It was very big. They went straight to his office.
"Here is the script."
"Thank you."
"Kindly study the script well and select a scene to do for me tomorrow."

Waheed entered with a smile and said, "Everybody in the studio said that you entered with a beautiful lady. So I assumed it was Kahraman. And here I am."
Kahraman smiled and said, "Thank you."
"This is Waheed," Salem said.
"Did you discuss everything with Salem?"
"Yes, but when is the opening?"
"It will be on the fifth of January. I guess I have finished my part. Now, it is your turn, Waheed. Excuse me. I have some work to do."
Salem left as Waheed turned to Kahraman.
"First thing I need you to do is to meet our costumes designer to select your costumes. We do not have much time left. As for

the other clothes in the movie, read the script and see what is required."
"Okay."
"Can you be here tomorrow morning at eleven?"
"Yes."
"I will practice with you the songs you have to dance for."
Kahraman nodded as he continued, "Any questions?"
"No."
"Then let us go and see the props."

Kahraman went with Waheed into a large hall that was filled with people working and preparing things. All of them stared at the lovely Kahraman. She smiled at everyone as Waheed introduced her to the crew.

"Dada, I have unexpected news."
"You are late. What has happened?"
"I'm going to act in a movie."
"Now, that is unexpected news."
"I know."
"Sit down and tell me the details."
"I have to go shopping, which reminds me, I will give you money to keep with you in case you need to buy something when I'm at work."
"God bless you, my love."

Next day, Kahraman did the scene she selected to the producer who found her a natural actress and that satisfied him. She then went to practice with Waheed. She tried to match the movements of her body to the rhythms of his music. They rehearsed for a long time. They heard each other's comments and worked on them. In the afternoons, she would go shopping with Hanan. At night, she would sit to study the script.

"What are you doing behind the door?"

"I want to try the costumes that were made for the movie."
"Show me when you finish."
She chose the colors red, white and black for the three costumes needed. She liked them very much. Hanan liked them much more than the costumes Kahraman wore in the club.

The time of the shooting had started. And Kahraman had to be in the studio at six in the morning to do her make-up and hair. A car would pick and drop her back everyday. It was the usual routine till the movie's production is finished. They would finish shooting at late night.

Kahraman became friends with all the crew that worked with her on the set. They all loved her. She was always on time. She sat with the make-up artist to learn more about how to apply make-up professionally. They both created a look for her face that would later be a trademark everywhere. Men would admire the look. Women would imitate her look. As for her hairdresser, she sat with him to style her hair in various styles.

One morning, when Kahraman left her apartment to go to the studio she heard her two neighbors talking about her again.

"Look at her, I wonder where she is going this early," one of the women said.
"Maybe to continue what she does at night," replied the other woman.
"It is strange that her grandmother is not chaperoning her."
"She does not need it. She has become a professional at what she does," the first woman ended sarcastically.

Kahraman ignored them and walked to the car. On the way, she told herself: "I will not listen to anyone. I will continue with what I'm doing. One day, I will be something, while they will remain as they are now. Also, I will change my house after I finish this movie. I know this is where my parents were living but I have no choice. I do not have to hear all this trash every single day of my life."

"I was wondering, do you mind if I use your music when I dance in the club?"
"It would be a great honor."
They chatted for some time then Kahraman excused herself.

"What is wrong, Dada?"
"I was thinking of something."
"What is it?"
"I'm happy that you have finished working in the movie. I hope it will be a success. I'm proud of you because you work hard. But do you know that what you're doing right now prevents you from doing other things."
"Like what?"
"Like getting married and having children."
"Dada, you worry too much. Thank you for all the love. But I'm not in hurry. I'm still young. I want to live my life. I'm happy with what I'm doing now. I want to continue my work. I have to wait for the right man who will take me and my career up and not down. Do you know what I mean, Dada?"
Hanan stared into her grand daughter's eyes and found countless dreams there that were longing to become true.
"Dada, I want to make a name of my own."

Kahraman was preparing herself for this important night. She chose a yellow gown that she had bought. Kahraman went to the studio where the make-up artist applied her fresh natural make-up. After that, her hairdresser started to style her hair for her. She was ready in time. Waheed and Salem came to pick her up from the studio. It was an unforgettable night for the dancer. There were several photographers taking pictures. The

camera flashes did not stop. Waheed held Kahraman's hand as they walked, while Kahraman smiled to everyone.
Kahraman watched herself carefully on the screen. She felt strange. "This is me, in front of all these people. And these people are watching me," she thought. But she was satisfied with her work for now. She knew she could be better in future. She felt proud of herself. She and the whole team were professional in what they did, especially Waheed. She loved his songs.
The movie finished. The lights were on. Waheed, Kahraman and Salem stood as fans surrounded them for autographs.

"Dada, I can never express how I feel."
"I'm sure it was a unique experience for you."
"It was, indeed."

Kahraman had a week to rest. She did not leave home. She relaxed, and tried to sleep as much as possible. She followed Hanan's advice on how to take care of her beauty. She applied special oil for her hair. To make it grow longer and to keep its shine after all the ironing they did. Also, she applied another oil just to keep her skin moist with a natural glow. Kahraman sat for hours grooming every day.

One evening, Hanan went out to buy some things she needed when her neighbor stopped her.
"Where is your night goddess? We have not seen her in days?"
Hanan left the woman talking and walked away from her.

"It is nice to get back to work here."
"The club and your customers missed you."
Nada came in.
"At last you are back."
"Here I am."
"Yes back to practice, girl."

Kahraman went to practice with Nada, but this time on Waheed's music that was taken from the movie.

Kahraman was back to her usual routine, attracting more and new customers every day. Her preparation with Nada extended more in terms of time. The only free time she had was in the morning which she spent mostly sleeping, but she liked her life as it was, and did not want to change it.

"Bye, Dada."
Kahraman left early to go for practice. On her way out she saw a cute girl playing with her toys on the stairs.
"Hello, cute one," Kahraman said with a smile.
The little girl moved away from Kahraman and said, "Mama told me not to speak to you."
"Why?"
"She said you are a bad girl."
Kahraman stared at the little girl for a second, then left.
"I'm going to move to another house. And it will be this week."

The movie 'My Love' was a huge hit. Many people were going to see it. Some people were seeing it for the second time. Kahraman and Waheed became the latest most admired couple in the movies. Kahraman was receiving a lot of letters every day from her fans. But she did not have the time to reply to each letter. She bought a huge box and kept the letters inside the box for remembrance. Late in the night, she would sit and read them with joy.

"Hello, Kahraman."
"Salem, it has been some time."
"I was busy working on some projects."
"You are here to see Salma?"
"I just dropped by to see you. Are you receiving your letters?"
"Yes. They are bringing them from the studio."

"Good. You did an excellent job. The movie is doing very well."
"I'm happy to hear that."

"Dada, I want to move to another house."
"You do not like the area anymore?"
"It is not the area, but the people that I do not like."
"The people are the same everywhere. But if that makes you happy then we will move to another house."
"This is where my parents lived. I love this home. I can still feel them around. But I have no choice."

Kahraman finished wearing her costume. She applied her make-up. And while she was brushing her hair, there was knock on the door.
"Yes?"
"Kahraman, it's me Waheed. Can I come in?"
She unlocked the door quickly.
"Why do you lock the door?"
"I do not like someone to enter while I'm getting prepared."
"I came to see you dance."
"Oh! You are welcome at any time. Have you seen Salma?"
"Actually, I have never met her before."
"Come, I will introduce you to her."

They went to Salma's office and sat with her for a while. Then Kahraman excused herself to go for her dance. Waheed and Salma sat in her booth.
"Nice booth you have here."
"Thank you."

"You are outstanding on stage."
"Thank you. I thought you had left."
"Go change. I will drop you back home."
"There is no need."
"I want to. Also, I want to talk to you about work."

Kahraman changed quickly and met Waheed outside.
"Let us go."
In his expensive car, Waheed continued speaking, "Are you interested in doing concerts with me?"
"Yes. That would be a nice concept."
"The first concert is next month in Cairo. Prepare yourself and I will advertise for your dance with me."
"I have to tell Salma first. Did you create any new songs?"
"I was busy doing concerts in several countries in the Middle East."
"I'm sure they were successful."
"Yes."
Finally, they arrived at Kahraman's house.
"Thank you for dropping me back home."
"I would like to see you tomorrow again. Will you have lunch with me?"
Kahraman smiled and said, "I would love that. Good night."

"Dada, I'm so happy."
"I can see your smile. I hope always. But what is the reason this time?"
"Waheed."
"Are you talking about Waheed the singer?"
"Yes. He dropped me back home. And he invited me to lunch tomorrow."
"Is it concerning work?"
"Yes and no."
"Explain."
"I'm going to be dancing in all of his concerts from now on. Also, he would like to see me tomorrow."
"Do you like him?"
"Ever since I saw him the first time but pushed the thought away since my work was a priority."

Waheed and Kahraman went to a restaurant that was close to the Nile River.
"You look very fresh, Kahraman."
"I feel fresh."
"I love your work. There is something special about you."
Kahraman stared into his eyes and said, "I want to be something."
"You are, Kahraman."
"I still have a long journey. I have many plans in mind."
"I can understand your ambition. And I would like to be part of it."
Kahraman was silent as he spoke again, "Do you mind?"
"No."
"Let me be closer to you."
Kahraman nodded as Waheed opened the menu.

"Salma, I wanted to tell you that I have a concert with Waheed next month."
"I will change the schedule and deal with everything."
"Thank you for your cooperation."

Within weeks, Kahraman had shifted to a new expensive furnished apartment. She preferred rented apartments from now on. She thought of buying a house and furnishing it beautifully in the future. Kahraman hired someone to help Hanan arrange things that were transferred to the new apartment, and hired a servant to do all the housework.

"Dada, I will be dancing in front of thousands of people in my first concert. I'm so excited."
"You will do fine. I know you."
Kahraman took all day to prepare for this concert.
"Kahraman, are you ready?" Waheed called from behind the door.
She opened the door and said, "Do I look okay?"

"Very pretty."
"Then I'm ready."
"Let us show them our best."

The concert lasted for two hours. Kahraman danced happily. The audience was very active. Many people took pictures of them. She loved his music and his voice. The dancer never forgot this night. It was an exception. This is her first concert with Waheed. But it was not her last concert. In the coming months, Kahraman was part of all Waheed's concerts.

Kahraman's life changed. Waheed filled her days and nights. They would spend all their free time together. She introduced him to Hanan. And when it came to work, they asked for each other's opinion. They even planned many things for the future. They decided to continue working together.

The couple was preparing for their next movie. Kahraman took her time to prepare a whole new wardrobe for the movie. She would sit with Waheed while he composed his songs. He asked her opinion in all his songs, as she asked his opinion in her dances. Then she exercised with his songs when they were finalized. She sat long hours to create new looks in make-up and hairstyles. It was weeks before they started shooting. Kahraman barely slept during the shooting days. She remained awake in the night to sit with Hanan and study her script. In the mornings, she would be in the make-up room by six and Salem would make sure everything was organized.

"You are exhausted, my dear."
"Yes."
"Since you are tired, enough reading."
"No. I have to finish these pages."
"Do you want something?"
"No. Thank you, Dada. Please go to sleep. It is very late."

Kahraman was the youngest dancer that earned the highest. She earned for her dancing in the club, the concerts and the movies. It was still the beginning for Kahraman. She was still only nineteen. Later, matters would change.

"Dada, I have added more money to your account."
"I already have too much."
"Go shopping. Buy things you like."
"Darling, I have everything."
"Buy more."
"Are you saving money?"
"Yes. Everything is under control. Do not worry."

The dancer set rules for her life, especially in work, and insisted on following each one of them:

Always be on time for any appointment.
Be prepared for anything at any time.
Practice dancing everyday.
Study the lines of the script very well.
The appearance should be perfect no matter what was her condition.
Never be satisfied with what is done.
Listen to other people's advice.
Make sure that no mistakes are done.
Think twice before doing or saying something.
Plan matters ahead of time.
Respect people who work with me.
Concentrate on what is being done.
Try to do the best.

The opening of her second movie was tonight. And Kahraman rested the day and prepared herself in mid afternoon.

It was time when both Waheed and Salem passed by to pick her up.
"You look very nice," Waheed said with a smile
They reached the opening ceremony that was filled with photographers. The couple stood as flashes popped around them. They looked perfect. Fit for one another. They went in and sat in their booth as the lights were turned off. And the movie started. There was silence. Everyone in the audience was watching. Kahraman stared at herself. She loved what she saw. But she knew she could still do better, as usual, never satisfied. In general, she loved the movie, especially Waheed. "You look lovely in that scene," Waheed whispered.

The new movie, 'I'm Yours', was a hit. Tickets were sold out in the first weeks of its release, adding to Waheed and Kahraman another success. Kahraman had new and more fans. She was receiving hundreds of letters each day. Kahraman met her fans from time to time. She kept distant in her activities from the public, and her life private.

"What next?"
"The next steps are several Dada."
"Have you not had enough?"
"Enough?" I have just started."

Salma advertised for Kahraman's comeback. And the tables in the club were booked in advance. She was earning a lot of money from Kahraman's popularity. She changed the stage décor, and prepared everything for her star to come back.

Kahraman danced in the club for the next few months, and continued practicing with Nada daily, as part of her usual routine. But Waheed had other plans. He wanted to take Kahraman to concerts outside Egypt. Kahraman loved the idea when Waheed told her.

"Dada, I will be traveling for a few weeks. I have concerts in the Middle East.
"What about the club?"
"They will change the program until I come back. Why don't you come with me?"
"I will wait here for you."

Kahraman and Waheed with his representative left for their trip to do the most successful concerts of the year. They toured in the Middle East and took advantage to visit the most important monuments in each country. Kahraman enjoyed every second of the trip with Waheed. Interviews of the famous couple were made in every country visited as well as photo shoots. The couple returned to Egypt after they finished their last concert.

"Dada, I missed you very much."
"I missed you a lot."
"I bought you gifts."
"Thank you, dear."
"I missed eating your food."
"It is ready and waiting for you."
"Tell me about your trip."
After a long chat, Kahraman slept.

The dancer was back at the club dancing. Salma changed many things for her star. Kahraman's dressing room was designed for a star. The stage was redesigned. The tables and chairs were increased since Salma had enlarged the hall to have more people per night. Kahraman was back to practice with Nada. But this time there was something new. She was also learning ballet with another teacher at the same time. She wanted to learn more and improve her muscle movement. Her aim was to blend dances together. The result would be something unique. Something no other dancer did at that time. She was eager to be different. And she was.

"I'm proud of you, Kahraman," Waheed said.
"Thank you, my love."
"You spend most of your time between two trainers. You are improving and dancing better."
"I still need time."
"I knew you were good since the first time I saw you. I have a surprise for you."
"What is it?"
"Not now. I will tell you later. It is a bit early."

The magazine was released with the couple's interview. And their picture was on the cover. The dancer never thought to collect what was written about her. But Hanan did so. Every morning she would pass by the bookstore and check. If there was anything concerning her granddaughter then she would buy it. She had made a huge collection for Kahraman.

"My dear, I'm very happy that you donated money to the poor children."
"I always wanted to do that, Dada."
"People will pray for you."

The magazines and newspapers wrote about the Kahraman's charity work. Everybody knew about the love relationship that was going on between her and Waheed. But everyone asked, 'Till when?' A question Hanan too asked herself secretly. Yet, she never approached her granddaughter about this issue. The couple was together for two years and a half. Waheed did not propose marriage. Kahraman was patient and waited.

Waheed's surprise to Kahraman was their third movie. She was thrilled. She loved the script after reading it. The actors that were going to act with them were a combination of the first and second movies. But this time, the producer was not Salem Shinawi. It was Ahmad Fawzi. He was one of the best producers in the country. Costumes were being prepared and training with Waheed on his songs began. She advised him to change some parts in his music so it would allow her to dance more fluently.

Waheed publicly dedicated all his songs to Kahraman. Many people envied the couple. They were one of the few couples that had lasted a long time together in the show business. Gossip was everywhere. But everything was still under control.

The shooting began and Kahraman was back to her usual tight schedule. She began to love acting but she missed what she does the best, dancing on stage. The scenes were taken in different parts of Egypt. The couple traveled to the locations and Kahraman missed her grandmother a lot.

Kahraman was back home, very exhausted. She slept for long hours, relaxed, and did not do anything for the first week. She always had a week off after each movie. She spent most of her time between Hanan and Waheed.
"You bought me a lot of presents, my love."
"You do not like them?"
"Of course, I do. But they are too much."
"Dada, if I could give you the world, then I would not wait a second."
"God bless you."
Hanan was worried about her granddaughter. She decided to wait before discussing her relationship with Waheed.

Kahraman had other plans on her mind that no one expected her to do. She was happy that her earnings were higher than before, which would help her in future to do what she had on her mind.

"I love you Kahraman, very much."
"And I love you, Waheed."
"I cannot live without you. You have become a part of me."
"I'm glad to hear that."
"Even in work. I cannot do anything without you. I trust you completely. You will stay with me forever?"
Kahraman was silent but Waheed did not notice her reaction, and gave her a box.
"Open it."
Kahraman opened the box to find a diamond bracelet.
"It is lovely. Thank you, habebe."

Kahraman was busy preparing herself for a photo shoot. She needed new pictures of herself for new promotional campaigns. She sat with the make-up artist and hairdresser to create a new look. She loved to change her appearance every now and then. Waheed adored the new pictures when he saw them. He took one picture that he liked the most. And Kahraman wrote on the back of it, 'You are the love of my life.'

The ballet that Kahraman was learning changed her dancing form completely. Her dancing was a blend of the Western and the Oriental styles. Many women tried to imitate the way she danced. The dancer thought of opening a school to teach all women how to dance. She asked a few people around her with regards to her idea and most agreed with her. In the next few months, Kahraman was busy finding the right location for her dancing school and started to furnish the place.

'Kahraman's Dancing School' was the name she chose for the school. It took a few months to be ready for the opening. The dancer chose the best dancing teachers she could find and advertised heavily in the media.

"Dada, please come for the opening of my dance school."
"You go enjoy your time."
"You will not change your mind?"
"My dear, get ready before it is too late."
Waheed accompanied Kahraman to the event along with Salima and others.

There were many journalists taking pictures of the famous couple and of the invites. Kahraman was ready to open her dance school. She was happy to see all the VIP guests in the opening invited by Salma. After the opening, she made a brief speech to her guests, which would be also sent to the press.

"I'm happy to be the first woman to open a dance school in the country. I hope that I'm not the last woman to open a dance school. I want every woman to learn how to dance. It is a must. It is part of her femininity. Thank you for coming and enjoy the rest of the evening."

"Congratulations Kahraman."
"Thank you Salma for inviting all the needed people to the event. I'm happy that Nada will be working between my club and your school."

Kahraman posed for the photographers alone and with other guests. She felt immense happiness but she was still not satisfied. There was more on her mind. And she was going to do every one of them.

The movie, 'You're my Life', was a success. The couple was happy that there work was appreciated. Waheed was considered one of the finest singers and Kahraman one of the most celebrated dancers.

But there was a time when Kahraman wanted to explode. The gossip concerning Waheed and her was increasing. Everybody was asking, 'When is the marriage?' It has been four years and a half. And Waheed did not propose. She had no answer to all the questions that people were asking her. She had to talk to him about it, but did not know how to bring up the subject.

"Kahraman, I want to talk to you about Waheed."
"I know what you are going to say, Dada."
"Then will you do something about it?"
"I will talk to him."

Kahraman danced in the club while Waheed sat watching her with Salma. He had a surprise for her. When Kahraman entered the room she found a huge bouquet of flowers with a card saying, 'Be my partner in our fourth movie.' She smiled and felt a mixture of happiness and disappointment. She changed and went to meet him.
"You don't seem to be happy with my surprise; you got bored of acting and dancing with me?"
"I never would."

Next day, Kahraman went to have lunch with Salma.
"I love the changes you did in the club."
"It was time. It has been a long time since I did something to it."
"I'm happy working with you, Salma and for being a friend of yours."
Salma smiled and said, "I feel the same towards you."
Kahraman then asked, "How did you open the club?"

"I was very young when I married an old rich man. Two years later he died, leaving me a lot of money. So I decided to open a club of my own."
"Why opening a club and not a boutique of clothes?"
"I wanted something that guarantees income. I wanted money. I did not want to go back to poverty. I was very poor when I was young."
"You did not have any brothers or sisters?"
"No."
"What about your parents?"
"They died."
"How did you meet your husband?"
"I was working for him."
"That is sweet of him."
"Yes. But he did not live long."
"Why didn't you remarry?"
"I did not meet anyone that was good as my husband."
Kahraman nodded as she ate. Then Salma asked, "When is your wedding to Waheed going to be?"
Kahraman was silent then quickly answered her, "Soon. Now we are busy doing our fourth movie together."
"I'm happy for you. You have been together for almost five years now. Take care of the people around you who gossip a lot."
"I know."

Kahraman's preparation for her fourth movie with Waheed is identical to the previous ones she has done before with him. She realized that there is not much difference or improvement to her as an actress from this movie or the previous ones. Her dancing became lighter and melodic thanks to his use of creative melodies and new music instruments but her acting abilities were frozen with these roles and Kahraman knew she could act better.

Months passed with a nervous Kahraman who could no longer bear this situation. On the other side, Waheed seemed unaware of anything around him. Kahraman was glad that the shooting of their movie was finished only waiting for the premier opening of the movie. Yet, she was happy that her dance school was doing very well under a professional team she hired to handle the school. The monthly reports showed how many women paid to be trained how to dance professionally.

One day, she was fed up of her situation and exploded on Waheed. Hanan was in her room listening to her granddaughter confronting Waheed.
"Till when are we going to stay like this?"
"What do you mean?"
"We have been in love for five years. And what is the end of this love?"
"There is no end, Kahraman."
"Yes, there is."
"What is wrong?"
"Everybody is asking me."
"Asking about what?"
"People are asking about our marriage!"
Waheed's face changed. And he said, "We are artists. We need to remain free to be creative."
"Are you saying that marrying me stops your creativity?"
"No. What I meant is that I want to marry my work to deliver my babies and that is my music to all the people."
"What about your personal life?"
"I'm happy with you the way I'm now."
"But I'm not."
"I'm sorry, Kahraman."
"I cannot remain like this."
"Then you chose the wrong man because I will never get married."
"That means you never loved me."

"I did. And I still do. Do not listen to what people around you are saying."
"I cannot."
"Is this how you want to end our love?"
"You're the one ending it."

Waheed had nothing to say especially when he saw Kahraman's persistence. He left her home while she stood next to the window to stare at him walking to his car. Hanan went to see her granddaughter. Tears were running down her cheeks.
"You were right, Dada."
"Do not cry, my love."
"Let me, Dada. I need to cry. It makes me feel better."
"He does not deserve your tears."
"I know. I'm not crying for losing him. I'm crying for the time I wasted in waiting for him to propose."
"You are still young. You will find someone else."
"I know that. And I will find someone."
Hanan hugged her granddaughter tightly.
"I'm hurt, but I'm strong. I will rise after this fall. No one will see me broken Dada."
"That is my Kahraman."
"I love you, Dada. Thank you for always being there for me. The only shoulder I will ever cry on."

Kahraman went to the opening of the movie with a diplomatic attitude so no one would notice anything. Photographers took pictures of the couple. They were the last pictures taken for them together. It was the end of doing films together. It was the end of their concerts together. What the couple did together would be a remembrance to all their fans. Kahraman sat between both men and watched the movie. She did not look at any side. She focused on the screen and thought, 'Will people remember my movies after years from now?' The movie was very good. She knew it would be a success. And she was right. The movie

'You Lied' was her final hit with Waheed and remained in the cinemas for a long time.

Next morning, her publicist issued the separation of the couple. There was an emptiness she could not tolerate. She decided to plunge into work more to exhaust herself to a stage she no longer has the energy to feel the emptiness.

Many changes were done in the next coming weeks. Kahraman changed all the music that she danced on. She brought a composer especially to compose music for her to dance to. She brought a new make-up artist and hairdresser to prepare her daily with a new fresh look. She brought a new fashion designer to design exclusively her dancing costumes and daily clothes to portray a mature woman. She brought a new photographer for her latest photo shoot to change her style of photography. And finally, Kahraman moved into a rented expensive furnished villa in a posh area with a small garden and a swimming pool.

The dancer started to wake up early every day for her classes of ballet and belly dancing classes with a new teacher. She met with the composer to listen to his music and to decide which she wanted to dance on. She passed by the dance school between time to time. She sat with the fashion designer for some time to sketch what she wanted. Some days she would squeeze her schedule more in order to meet her publicist and agent.

In the following weeks, her agent called to inform Kahraman that a producer wanted her to act in his latest movie. The dancer accepted after she had read the script. She sat with the producer Saif, in her agent's office and discussed details. Actor Nader Nabelsi would be starring with her in the movie. He was one of the most popular actors in the country. And Kahraman liked the idea of working with him.

The next day, Nader came to the club to watch Kahraman dance. He instantly fell head over heels in love with her performance.

When she finished her dance, Kahraman was introduced to him by Saif.

"I love the way you dance," the actor commented.
"Thank you."
"It is my first time to work with both of you and I'm looking forward to it," said Saif.
"I'm sure that Kahraman is easy to work with," said Nader.
"You will love working with Kahraman. She is a hard worker. And gives you quality in everything she does," replied Salma.
They had a snack and talked for some time. Then Nader insisted on dropping Kahraman back home.

Kahraman had a month and a half to prepare herself for the shooting. Nader was a regular visitor to the club, sending the dancer flowers every day and not any color, only yellow and red, the first for jealousy and the second for passion to express what sort of man he was. Kahraman recognized his admiration but was not ready for another disappointment. She accepted going out with him in her free time.

Both her agent and spokesman tried to convince her to do more interviews, she flatly refused. The dancer disliked doing interviews. She had plans on her mind to do and none of the people around her knew what she was planning.

The shooting for the movie began. Kahraman paid close attention to Saif instructions and kept a diplomatic relationship with her co-star.

"Why are pushing me away?" he asked.
"I am not. I am just not ready for any relationship."
"Give me a chance."
"I prefer to stay friends for the time being."
"I'm not Waheed."
"No one knows anything about my relationship with Waheed!"

"The moment you think that you've learned enough. You will find yourself declining. And fast."

ঔ

"When something is broken to pieces, it could be fixed, but it will never be beautiful again."

ঔ

"I would never love anyone that perceives my work as a disgrace."

ঔ

"I want to constantly reinvent myself so I do not get bored with myself and so will the people around me."

ঔ

"I want to be accepted as a professional belly dancer and as a lady."

ঔ

In the coming days, Nader arranged to send Kahraman breakfast to her room in the studio with flowers. At lunchtime, he would invite her to delicious restaurants. Everybody on the set knew that Nader is infatuated by Kahraman.

"Dada, I do not know how to explain things."
"Try."
Kahraman told her everything Nader did to her daily.
"You are not exaggerating?"
"No, Dada. That is why I do not know how to explain."

"He is infatuated by you. Take care; you do not want to be hurt again."
"I know."

In the coming weeks, Kahraman finished shooting her fifth movie. She was glad it was out of her daily schedule since she had several matters to do. She donated a large sum of money to all the renowned orphanages in the country. Also, she sent children toys as well as visiting these orphanages and spending time with the children, playing and talking to them. Kahraman enjoyed every second of these days. She loved these children and took photos for remembrance.

The news was splashed everywhere. The pictures were released with a small text prepared by her spokesman. Many journalists tried to do interviews with the dancer but her spokesman declined. It was Kahraman's orders. In her personal life, Nader was like her shadow that supported her vision and encouraged her further to pursue it. He was introduced to Hanan who liked him. Everybody around Kahraman liked Nader, who was good to everyone who treated Kahraman well.

Tonight, was the premier night of the movie, welcomed by the media and fans, the stars moved to their booth to meet the producer before the movie begin.

"I love your dancing in that part," he whispered.
And Kahraman whispered back, "And I love you in every part of the movie."
Nader stared into Kahraman's eyes for a few seconds, shocked from what she had said. She never told him anything like that before.

Kahraman was falling in love with Nader. She could not find any fault with his behavior. He treated her very well. No one made her feel special and important as he did. But she was afraid of one thing. "What would be the end of this love?"

The dancer started to prepare herself for her first solo concerts in Egypt. She took few months off from the club to design the concerts concept and its promotional campaign.

"I want to come with you everywhere."
"I will be traveling to different cities!"
"I want to be with you."

Kahraman was excited to see large audiences at every concert. Nader accompanied her throughout her tour which lasted a few weeks. In her free time, after rehearsals, the couple spent time on beaches, parks or restaurants to know each other further. After the tour was over, the couple returned to Cairo.

"Why not take a vacation?"
"This is my prime time dada. I will not waste a minute of it. One day it will be all over, especially when I become old."
"You will always be pretty."
"That is because you love me. But not everyone will think the way you do."

On Friday, Nader invited Kahraman to dinner in a fancy restaurant.
"I want you to take a month off."
"Why?"
"But you can if I ask you to do so?"
"It depends for what reason."
"It is a good reason. I assure you."
"What is it?"
"Earlier in the car, you said you have a surprise to tell me about, what is it?"
"I am going to open a school for children."

"Is the education for free?"
"Yes."
"You love children to that degree?"
"Very."
"I'm proud of you Kahraman and I'm right behind you in any decision you take."
Kahraman's eyes were filled with tears and excused to go to the restroom as Nader ordered food.
"I ordered food."
Kahraman nodded as she took her glass of champagne for a sip when she noticed a huge diamond ring in it. Her eyes moved from the ring to Nader with surprise.
"I'm madly in love with you. Will you marry me?"
He took the ring out of the glass, dried it, and placed it on Kahraman's finger. "Keep it on your finger and think about it. But do not let me wait long."
Kahraman felt happiness beyond measures. She did not know what to say until he continued, "But you will have to stop working once you marry me."
Without any thought Kahraman took the ring off and placed it in his hand.
"Why?"
"I will not leave my work for any reason now."
"Not even for me?"
"Not even for you."
Nader was silent for seconds as Kahraman continued, "You either marry me as I'm or forget about me completely."
"Let me think about it."
Nader tried to create a romantic atmosphere again but Kahraman was somewhere else. She was worried. Countless questions crossed Kahraman's mind. For several seconds, she was elsewhere then was back to reality.
"I' am sorry but I suddenly feel tired and would like to go home."
"But you did not eat anything!"

"I'm not hungry."

On the way Nader held her hand till they arrived to her home.
"Good night Nader."
"Good night Kahraman." She walked towards the door without looking back. When she entered home Hanan realized how her granddaughter's face was pale.
"Did you enjoy your time?"
"In the beginning only."
"What is the matter dear?"
"Nader proposed to me."
"I'm happy for you. That is good news."
"It is not."
"Why?"
"Because he wants me to leave work if I marry him."
"And would you?"
"No dada. I worked hard to reach where I'm now. I will not."
"Did you tell him that?"
"Yes. And I told him that if he wants me then he will have to take me as I' am."
"What was his reply?"
"He will think about it. It is funny. Men usually wait for the answer of women. In my case it is the opposite." Kahraman laughed sarcastically.
Hanan felt sad for her granddaughter but knew that she had a point.

Kahraman could not sleep that night. She sat in front of the window watching sunrise. Hanan woke up early for prayers and found Kahraman sitting.

"You did not sleep?"
"No. It is good that you are awake. I wanted to talk to someone."
"Tell me what is on your mind?"

"I want to open a school for children."
"That is a wonderful idea."
"After sometime I will go with my agent to search for a place that will be suitable for the school."
"I'm very proud of you. I wish your father was alive to see what you are doing."

Kahraman was keen on finding a land for the school quickly. She went with her agent to see several different areas. She found the perfect location for her school. Her agent would finalize the purchase of the land. Also, assigned a professional to build and design the school. It would take some time till it is ready. Finally she hired the best school manager in the country to handle her school, giving complete authority to choose the teachers and the books that were to be taught to the children.

"How did things go on my dear?"
"Bought the location, assigned professionals to build and design the school and the principle."
"You never waste time. That is a very good habit you inherited from your father. Nader passed by to see you and waited for sometime then left."
"It is okay. I will see him tomorrow. Now I have to go the club."

The dancer met her audience with a wide smile. She focused on her dancing and forgot all her worries, especially when she heard the audience clapping for several minutes. When she finished, Kahraman found Nader waiting back stage.
"I did not know you were coming."
"I missed you. Change and I will wait for you in Salma's office."
Kahraman changed her costume and was out in minutes. On their way home, Nader started talking.
"May I request you to act with me in my next movie? The script is with me. Read it and let me know."
"Fine, I will take a look at it tonight."

Then there was a long silence before he spoke again when they reached in front of her house.
"Thank you. I love you Kahraman."
Kahraman entered home to find Hanan sitting in the living room.
"I hope everything is alright?"
"Nothing much happened. Except that I was given a script to read."
"Are you hungry?"
"No dada. Thank you. I will sit and read the script. Try to sleep."
"If you want anything then wake me up. Good night."
Kahraman changed her clothes and sat reading. After a long time of reading, she found the script very good.

In the coming months, Kahraman finished studying the script, preparing herself for the movie yet keeping an eye on both of her projects. The shooting started and Kahraman was pushing herself to extremes. She wanted to test her degree of resistance towards exhaustion. The relationship between them was not as it once was. Nader hoped to tempt her to change her decision. He miscalculated Kahraman's way of thinking. She would never yield to any man's desire.

Between her publicist and agent, Kahraman worked on her personal projects. She was glad to know that the children's school was almost ready and went personally to see it. Advertisement of the school was released in the media.

Another shocking reaction by the media and the people, "How could a belly dancer open a children school, when she is not educated herself?" Kahraman expected a negative reaction and prepared a reply to the media and the people who will attend the opening. It said:

"I love children. And I'm trying my best to help them in every possible way. I want all the children of my country to be well educated. So they would be useful to their society. I opened this school especially to help them gain good education as a base for a higher education. The school fees are for free as a gift from me to all the children. The school will be directed by a group of professional that were chosen carefully. I wish all my children the best of luck. And I hope to see them as important people in the near future."

The dancer went for the opening of her school in high spirits. There was a huge crowd of people, and media. Kahraman cut the ribbon to let everyone in to see the school. She was photographed with some of the school staff, her agent, her spokesman, and some guests. But she refused to do any interviews. Kahraman was very pleased with her third personal achievement.

Nader made up his mind and decided to talk to Kahraman.
"Please change your mind. Marry me. You do not need to work. I will get you everything you need."
"I'm sorry. I repeat again. I cannot leave my work."
"I love you very much."
"Then marry me as I'm now."
"I cannot."
"Why what is wrong with me working?"
"People will say I married 'The Dancer'."
Kahraman was furious and answered in a very cold manner, "Then I see I am wasting my time."
"What about our love?"
Without a reply, Kahraman walked away.

Kahraman no longer felt sad after the conversation that went between Nader and herself. "I do not need man like that."

"What happened?"

"As expected, he refused to marry me if I keep on working."
"Won't you leave your work for him?"
"You know me by now dada. I will never leave my work for any man."
"But he loves you."
"Many men will love me. But I want one that respects me and my work."
"Do you think you will find someone like that?"
"I hope so."
"You won't change your mind?"
"No."

One morning her agent introduced her to celebrated photographer Nabil Fany.
"I am delighted to meet you Kahraman."
"The pleasure is mine. I have heard about your outstanding work."
"I' am happy to know that. I came last week to Salma's club and saw you dancing. I have to admit that I fell in love with your dancing."
"Thank you very much"
"I would like to take live photos of you."
"I do not mind at all. I would love to be photographed by one of the most celebrated photographers in the country."

In the next few weeks, Kahraman was busy taking countless photos with Nabil. He took live pictures of her on stage while dancing. In the studio as she was getting ready for her performance. He took pictures of her in swimming pools, gardens, and while exercising. The purpose of these photos was to capture the natural essence of Kahraman. She felt satisfaction when Nabil gave her the pictures. She gave them to her agent to distribute them with the news of her concerts throughout the Middle East; also, the dancer selected her favorites and placed them in her dancing school.

"What do you think dada?"
"They are all nice. It is very hard to choose any of them."
"I know."
"Tell me when are you traveling?"
"Next week. Nabil is coming with me. He will take a lot of pictures of me there. He said there are very beautiful backgrounds that we should not miss in the other countries. And I think he is right."
"I would like to meet him before you leave."
"I invited him today to come here in the afternoon."
"Good."
"Are you worried about me dada?"
"I'm always worried."
"Don't worry my dear. I can take care of myself."

Nabil came to Kahraman's house, met Hanan and enjoyed their company. In the coming days, Kahraman prepared herself for the three week trip. Nabil took pictures of her in every country they visited. Her concerts were a massive success. Nabil heard about her projects but did not believe that they were good enough until she explained to him the concept of each. He found her extremely dedicated to her work, and had no time for gossip as the rest of the belly dancers he worked with. She was busy making a name of her own. His respect to her increased and in his eyes, he saw a lady.

"Dada, what do you think of the new pictures?"
"They are all very pretty."
"I'm very happy dada. The concerts were a great success."
"I'm glad to hear that."
"How is Nabil with you?"
"We are friends. He wants to see the schools, so will take him to see them."
"Is there a possibility for a love relationship?"

"No."

Nabil watched Kahraman practice for hours.
"I did not know it was hard work."
"It is but I love my work."
Kahraman took a hot shower and got dressed in a simple black dress with big black glasses, a short black wig and a scarf.
"I do not want anyone to recognize me. Let us go for a drink."
The café was close to Salma's club, so they went walking.

Kahraman's photos were printed on postcards and posters to be sold in the market. The selected photos were the ones in the bathtub, getting dressed or in her sleeping attire. The sensual and seductive photos caused a stir in Egypt as well as in the Middle East, making Kahraman cross the red lines without any thought. No celebrity dared to do what she did. Her brief reply was:

"There is no harm in being creative. Creativity knows no traditions or red lines. And I want to be creative in everything I do."

Since her sixth movie "Honey" was a success, several producers sent the dancer scripts to read. She found them either repetitive of her previous roles or just commercial, so she declined all of them. She wanted a powerful script and knew that something good will come up. She simply had to wait.

In the meantime, Nabil taught Kahraman some photography techniques. He showed her which lightning suits her and which doesn't. He taught her to pose in different forms and how to deal with the camera in a more natural manner. She was a good listener that grasped details easily.

She returned home in the evening and found no one in the house. She called for Hanan and the servant but there was no response. Kahraman knew that Hanan would never leave the house at that time. She did not tell her today at lunch that she was going out. Nadia was supposed to be in the house all the time. She waited for sometime in case they showed up then called Salma, told her she's not coming tonight, and called Nabil. They waited for some time until Kahraman lost her patience and said, "Will call the police."
"Let me do all the talking."

The police came to her house to search for clues but did not find any. It was late midnight, and there was no sign of them.
"They have been kidnapped." said the inspector.
"What do we do now?" asked Nabil.
"First step is to guard the house so that nothing happens to Kahraman in case some of them came back. Some police men will stay day and night protecting the house. The next step is that Kahraman should never leave the house. You have to wait for their phone call. They might call in any minute. The third step is that you should inform us with everything that happens between you and them. The fourth step is that you should never do anything they say without consulting us." added the inspector.
"How long will it take?" asked Kahraman worriedly.
"It usually doesn't take much time since they are after money." finished the inspector.
Kahraman sat on the couch and burst into tears. Salma and Nada came to see Kahraman after the club closed.
"Thank you for coming. Can you both sleep here? I'm afraid to be alone."
"Of course we will." said Salma.
"Thank you. I will never forget your support."
They all sat waiting next to the phone.

"I will do some fresh lemonade to calm your nerves Kahraman." said Nada.

Next morning the news splashed everywhere in the country. Her spokesman dealt with everything in order not to bother Kahraman. The media tried to reach Kahraman who remained hidden in her house and refused to speak to anyone. Her case became the most talked about in the coming days.

The kidnappers called again to give her details of time, place and rules for giving the money. The police was on standby as she went with the bag of money following their instructions. She waited for sometime but no one showed up again. Kahraman went back to the car furious with hot tears running down her cheeks. As soon as she reached home, the phone was ringing.

"Do you still want her?"
"Yes. Please. Do not harm her."
"Do not tell us what to do."
"Can I hear her voice?"
"No."
"When will we meet?"
"I will call you. Wait."

The man hung up leaving Kahraman screaming. Salma and Nada helped her to the room. Nabil called to inform the inspector.

"We are getting close to the end of it." said the inspector.
"How do you know?" Nabil asked.
"They set two appointments to meet with them and did not show up. I think they want her to suffer for a while. Time is running. They will soon call again for another appointment. They need the money. They cannot wait much longer. You'll see."

The inspector was right. After a few days they called again.
"Be ready in the same place and time. We will be in a large brown boat in the middle of the Nile River. Come in a small boat. No company. Get it?"
"Yes."
"You better have the money."
"It will be with me."

The man hung up. But Kahraman stood staring at the phone, scared that they might not come again. She was beginning to lose hope. Nabil called the inspector to update him. The police were ready. They surrounded the Nile River with armed policemen that were in groups on small boats hiding between the plants in different parts in the Nile River. Kahraman sat in the boat and started to row till she reached the brown boat. There was a policeman under her wooden seat. She was very scared, tensed, and worried but tried her best to look cool and calm. There was a man standing on the deck.

"Come closer."
She moved the boat a bit close and said, "I'm close. Show me Hanan."
The man gave a sign to other men to bring her on the deck. Finally Kahraman saw Hanan.
"Where is the money?"
Kahraman pushed the bag towards them. The man opened them to check and nodded.
"Now give me Hanan."
"No. For a second thought I changed my mind."
"What?"
The police man under the wooden seat showed up with a gun, pushing Kahraman back in the boat. Within seconds, the kidnapper's boat was surrounded by police boats. Now they stood in front of each other with guns pointed towards one another.

"Drop your gun." The policeman ordered.
"Didn't I say no company? Now, you will never see your grandmother again in your life."
"The police are surrounding you. There is no way to escape. Drop your gun. Or I will shoot."

The man moved quickly to hold Hanan but the policeman shot him in the arm in a second. The man fell. His men surrounded him and held Hanan who was crying from fear. Kahraman was at the back of the boat staring with fear to what was happening.
"Surrender now. There is no way to run anywhere." said the policeman.

The group of kidnappers knew they were surrounded but insisted on not giving Hanan and Nadia to them. They remained for some time till they surrendered. Hanan and Nadia rushed freely to Kahraman as the police took care of everything. Kahraman, Hanan, and Nadia rode back to the shore on another boat and met with Nabil, Salma, and Nada at the shore then they all went home.

The case was over and everything went back to normal. The press tried to reach Kahraman who maintained a distance for sometime. In the coming days, Kahraman moved into another house and kept a guard to protect the house as well as one to accompany her on daily basis. The incident would not be mentioned again.

Kahraman decided to take a month off to spend time with Hanan. She wanted to regain all the time she lost away from Hanan. She insisted on taking Hanan for a complete medical check up and Hanan advised Kahraman to do the same.

Three days later, the doctor called Kahraman and asked her to come to the hospital for the results.

"Hanan is in very good shape. There is nothing to worry about."
"As for you, everything is alright except for one thing."
"What is it Doctor?"
"You are unable to conceive any children."
Kahraman froze for minutes, shocked, then asked, "Why?"
The doctor explained in details her case until she grasped it and added, "You can check with other doctors for another opinion but I will be honest with you, it will be a waste of time. I'm sorry Kahraman. There is nothing I can do."
Tears formed in her eyes as she said, "Kindly, do not tell any one."
"It is strictly confidential. Do not worry."
"Thank you doctor."
Kahraman put on her dark black glasses and left. In the car, she cried silently.

"What is wrong my dear?"
"I took the result of your tests and thank God you are in good health as well as mine, except that I cannot conceive children!"
Hanan hugged her granddaughter as she cried her heart out.
"Do you want to consult another doctor?"
"No. The doctor we went to is the best in the country."
"My dear, do not tell anyone about this."
"I will not. It is something hurtful to talk about."

Kahraman canceled all her shows in the club for the time being, saying she's not feeling well and it was the doctor's instructions. She did not leave her house in the coming weeks. She refused to speak or meet anyone. Her life froze to this stage.

"Why? Why me? Now what am I to do? Accept that horrible fact just like that? It seems so. But I feel I am like a dead tree standing alone."

After weeks have passed, Hanan could no longer tolerate the situation and spoke to her granddaughter bluntly.
"Dry your tears my dear, they won't help you. I know it is hard but you have to accept that fact."
"I cannot."
"You will have to, because you can not do anything about it. God has given you almost everything but no one can have everything. Nobody's perfect. Stand in front of the mirror. See yourself. You lost weight and you look very pale."

Hanan opened the curtains to allow light to fill the room that was dark for weeks. Kahraman closed her eyes unable to bear the rays of light. She got use to the darkness. Then Hanan pulled her granddaughter out of the bed towards the mirror. Kahraman saw her pale face and slim figure for the first time in weeks. For the next coming days, Kahraman thanked the people who sent her flowers and apologized for not replying to their calls, started to eat again to gain the weight she lost and pampered herself. Eventually, Kahraman went back to dancing in Salma's Club but this time for only two nights a week.

Her agent sent her another script that might appeal to her and it did. She was the only star in the movie in addition to supporting actors. The producer was a newcomer that wanted Kahraman in her second movie. Her agent advised her not to take the risk, but Kahraman wanted to help a rising female producer and accepted saying, "I think women should stick together. Don't you think?"

The dancer began working on her seventh movie as she also worked on other new projects for the next few months. She barely had time to check on all of her projects and hired a professional to handle her personal projects completely. Kahraman decided to open a house to take care of all the unwanted children in the country and refused to call it an 'orphanage'. She would name it as 'Kahraman's House'. Also, to open a recruitment office to help women find jobs.

One evening, Kahraman made a gathering for all her close friends to spend an enjoyable time with them. The dancer met Nabil one morning for breakfast to ask his opinion regarding a small project.

"I was thinking of releasing a book that includes my pictures with a short brief about me and you will take these photos. What do you think?"

"It is a great idea. We must select the best photos."

"I agree."

"Also, we need new photos that will be exclusively taken and released for this book."

"Do you have any ideas?"

"Yes, we will visit several cities in Egypt that are not commonly popular for photo shoots and arrange them to be the perfect spots for photo shoots."

"I believe we have the base set for our up coming project that we will begin implementing after I finish the movie."

In her free time, Kahraman visited her dance school as well as her educational school to make sure they are running smoothly and the location of her two new upcoming projects to see the final steps towards opening.

The recruitment office to find jobs for women was in the name of the dancer and the opening of it was mid-morning. Kahraman with her supporters arrived to the opening where media gathered as well as some VIP guests. In the same week was the opening of her seventh movie. Kahraman barely had time to rest as her other project; Kahraman's House was to be opened in a week's time. The dancer was talk of the country by her deeds and released a short quote:

"I know I'm not the first person to come up with the idea and not the last one, but in my case it is different. I refuse to call it an orphanage. It will be a house, my house. Given and dedicated to all the unwanted children. If they are unwanted by their parents then I will take care of them. I will take care of each child in my house. They will be my children. And I will be their mother. I will make sure that they are raised properly. I'm trying to help these children so please help me in return for the sake of our children."

Kahraman was no ordinary woman any more. She was becoming an important figure. Not as a belly dancer, but as a business woman who did many things to her country. Yet, there were still people from the society who refused to accept her no matter what she did.

"Dada I'm happy for my children."
"God bless you for helping them. I believe you need to take a break from projects."
"Yes for the time being."
"Darling I'm worried about you financially."
"Don't worry; my accountant is keeping everything in order."
"What is next?"
"I will be doing a book with my pictures."
"Do you guarantee an income from it?"
"Yes. I will travel after two weeks around Egypt for the photo shoots."
"What about the club?"
"I will dance for two weeks then travel. I have to inform Salma about it."

Kahraman invited Salma to the pool in her house and for lunch then the dancer consulted Salma on her up coming 'book' project. The club owner encouraged her to go ahead and Kahraman asked for few advises.

The dancer traveled with her team of professionals to several cities in Egypt with Nabil. Kahraman was fascinated by the nature she saw and by the warm welcome she has received from the villagers. A glorious two weeks left the dancer content and relaxed. She returned to Cairo with lots of stories to tell her grandmother and friends.

"Dada, I have to take you to these villages. They are simply mesmerizing."
"I am too old to travel my dear."

The movie 'The Dancer' was a success that Kahraman did not expect. The movie remained for weeks in the cinema, adding more income to the star's bank account as she takes a percentage from the tickets sale. In the coming days, the photos were in front of Kahraman and they were fabulous. She and Nabil chose the best ones for the book. They decided not to include any of the old photos. The book would show the heritage of Egypt through Kahraman's eyes. Her agent was to deal with all publishing and distribution issues.

Within two months, the book's layout was made and published. It was sold in all bookstores, street markets, and tourist destinations in Egypt. It was sold out in the first week of its release just like the postcards. More copies were issued to be printed again. Kahraman was becoming a rich business woman that earned more than men did at the time. None of her projects were a failure which encouraged her to have open ears for new projects.

Kahraman couldn't sleep at times especially when she thought of children. She would sit in the living room staring at the moon. She tried her best not to make any noises so her grandmother would not wake up but Hanan was a light sleeper and felt her granddaughter awake.

"My dear, why are you not asleep?"
"I'm thinking dada. I can not sleep."
"Tell me."
"Which man will marry me now?"
"You will find someone my dear. Do not worry. It is fate."
"I'm scared dada. I do not want to spend the rest of my life alone."
"You will not. I'm always next to you."
"I love you dada."
"Sleep my love."

Fareed Fahmi was sitting with his friends in a booth close to the stage. The music started, the lights turned on, and the curtains opened to reveal the lovely Kahraman. She moved her body like a light feather. Her eye spotted a group of men sitting in the first booth. She smiled and moved away to the center.

When the dancer finished her show for tonight and went to change there was a knock on the door.
"Yes?"
"It's me Salma."
Kahraman unlocked the door.
"I want to introduce you to a group of writers and producers."
"Okay. Give me ten minutes."
She arranged herself quickly and went out.

"Good evening gentlemen." Kahraman said. All the men stood up instantly to greet her. Each one of them introduced himself. Kahraman was seated next to Fareed Fahmi as they chatted till late night about various topics.

"You're very late my dear."

"I' am sorry Dada. I met an interesting man through Salma."
"Who is he?"
"Farid Fahmi."
"Is he the author?"
"Yes. You know him?"
"I heard a lot about him, known to be highly educated and a renowned author."
"Also, I was introduced to script writers and producers. Their conversations are extremely interesting."
"In what way is their conversation different?"
"They talked about writing scripts and books structures, acting methods and stage production."
"I'm happy you met such intelligent people."
"I admit that I admired Farid Fahmi in particular."
"And what did you like about him?"
"The topics he tackled in conversation were impressive."

In the next few weeks Fareed and his group were regular visitors to Salma's club. He sat with his friends to watch Kahraman dance. Kahraman sat with them every time they came to the club. On one night, Fareed asked, "One of the plays I wrote will be acted on stage tomorrow. Are you interested to see one?"
"Very much." replied Kahraman.
Kahraman returned home filled with anxiousness, rushing to tell her grandmother.
"He invited me to the theater tomorrow."
"I have never seen you this excited."
"After sitting with him several times, I know that I want this man for a husband."

That night Kahraman slept peacefully. The next day, she got ready early and left early to make sure she arrives on time in case there was traffic.

"What do you expect from my play?"

"I expect something complex and dramatic."
"I guess you chose the right words. I hope you enjoy watching it."
"I'm sure I will. It is my first time to see a play acted on stage."
"It is a different experience."

When they arrived to the theater there were a lot of people attending the play. There were critics, authors, poets and journalists. No one expected to see Kahraman there and especially with Fareed Fahmi. Kahraman sat in the front row next to Fareed. Everybody was staring at them. She realized how many important figures were watching his play. The play started on time. The dancer watched intently focusing on every single detail. She was right when she categorized his work. It was very complex but she loved the complexity. Fareed observed Kahraman from the corner of his eye. She was glad when everyone stood and applauded after the play ended. For a split second, she felt it was for her.

"Indeed a different experience. I'm looking forward to reading your books."
"Do you like to read?"
"I never had the time or even thought of it."
"I can understand your busy schedule. I have heard a lot about your interesting projects."
"If you like I can be a guide and show you everything."
"Let me know when you are free to take me."
"Thank you for sharing with me such an important moment in your life."
"The pleasure is mine Kahraman."

"How was it?"
"Dada I told you he is the one for me."
"How could you be sure?"
"I feel I am a pebble in his ocean when with him."

In the coming days, Kahraman took Fareed to show him her projects. He liked what he saw and what he heard. He instantly fell in love with her work as a business lady apart from the magical performances she made on stage.

"I'm fascinated by what you are doing."
"I still have other projects in mind but I want to keep them a surprise." added Kahraman.
"More? Like what?"
"I will not reveal anything before it's time."
"How old are you?"
"That is not a question to ask a woman!" joked Kahraman.
"That is not just any woman but a lady. Not just any lady, my lady."
Kahraman was shocked for a second before she smiled softly.
"No plans for marriage. What are you waiting?"
"I have been waiting for a gentleman like you."
Fareed smiled gently and kissed her hands lightly.

In the next months, Kahraman was busy reading the books that Fareed wrote. She admired his style of writing. Fareed took Kahraman to places she never thought of going to such as museums, and historical monuments. After months, Fareed invited Kahraman to meet his parents.

"Dada he wants me to meet his parents."
"That means he loves and respects you very much."
"Dada, what if he asked me to marry him? What will I tell him about the children factor?"
"If he loves you then he will accept you as you are."
"That depends how much he will love me."

Kahraman reached to an old villa that looked antique. She loved what she saw and the surroundings. The door was open and an old couple stood there.

"Good afternoon" greeted Fareed as he hugged his mother and then turned to his father.
"How are you son?"
"I'm fine dad."
"I would like both of you to meet Kahraman."
"Come in my dear" urged his mother.

They entered straight to the living room. Kahraman stared around her to find a very cosy atmosphere, she instantly felt home. She sat listening to the family conversation. She felt comfortable between them but Kahraman was nervous. She did not know what topics to talk about, felt shy and hesitant.

Fareed went with his father to the library leaving his mother with Kahraman.
"I see a lot of pictures of you but you look prettier in person."
"That is sweet of you."
"I'm very sorry about your grandmother. Hope she recovered."
"Yes she did and I thank you for your concern."
"You live alone with your grandmother?"
"Yes. Actually Fareed will meet my grandmother tomorrow. You are most welcome to come."
"We won't be able to make it tomorrow but we can make it some other time. I have to prepare dinner. I will be back soon."
"I would like to help you."
"You are my guest."
"Kindly let me help."
"If you insist then fine."
Kahraman followed his mother to the kitchen.
"Do you cook?"
Kahraman felt embarrassed and said, "No."

"That is not a problem. You can learn easily."
"Is it easy?"
"Yes. Do not worry about that."
Kahraman helped her arrange the table then called Fareed and his father to the table. They sat and ate. There was silence until his father talked, "How are your projects going?"
"The projects are doing extremely well. I took Fareed to see them."
"I'm very interested in your projects."
"Thank you. If you like, I can take you to see them?"
"That would be great."
They continued chatting about politics and economy. Kahraman listened silently and did not interact in the conversation. She barely knew about politics or economy and the lack of it embarrassed her. In that second, she decided to read the newspaper everyday and discuss politics or economy with Fareed. After dinner, they went to the tearoom, and continued their conversation until Fareed asked her, "Ready?"
"Yes."
"Stay more" insisted his mother.
"I'm sorry. I have my show that will start in two hours from now."
"Do you dance every night?" His father asked.
"Yes. But If I have other projects then I can cancel it."
"Good luck my dear." His parents said.

The couple left the house and was heading to Kahraman's residence. She was silent on the way.

"Why are you silent?"
"I apologize. I am just nervous."
"And shy?"
Kahraman smiled lightly and said, "Yes, but I loved your parents."
"And they loved you."

"Not a compliment?"
"No. My father wouldn't have said he wanted to see your projects or my mother wouldn't have insisted on you to stay."
"Thank you for giving me the chance to meet your parents. Tomorrow you're invited to meet my grandmother. I asked your mother if they could come but she said they will not be able to come."
"They have to attend a friend's funeral."
"Sweet Fareed, good night."
"My precious Kahraman, sleep well."

As soon as she entered the house, Hanan asked, "How did it go?"
"Where should I start from?"
"Start from the moment he picked you up." Kahraman told her grandmother all the juicy details before sleeping.

Next morning, Kahraman ordered Nadia to buy her the newspaper for her every morning. She had her breakfast in the garden and read the newspaper in details. She had several questions to ask Fareed when he comes concerning politics. In the afternoon, Fareed arrived to meet Hanan. They chatted for a while before lunch. After lunch, Kahraman asked him her questions regarding politics and economy?"
"Why do you want to know?"
"I want to know more about politics because it is a segment that defines the situation of nations as for knowing more about economy, I want to be a successful business woman, and I must have some basic knowledge in the economy of my country to begin with."
"Impressed Kahraman." said Fareed as he answered her questions.
Kahraman showed him around the house and Fareed said, "I love the way your house is designed. Did you design it?"

"That is why I rented it. I liked it myself but I'm planning to buy a house of my own."
"I believe you made a mistake for opening these projects before buying a house of your own. You must have a home of your own."
"You have a point."

Kahraman excused herself to get ready for her show in the club leaving Hanan with Fareed talking. After half an hour Kahraman came out and said, "How about both of you come to the club with me?"

Hanan never minded any of the men her granddaughter got involved with but Fareed was the only man she really wanted her granddaughter to marry. For the first, Hanan accepted to go to the club since Fareed will keep her company.

Kahraman picked Fareed's parents and took them for a tour around her projects then invited them to meet her grandmother who was delighted. Fareed joined them later in the afternoon. Kahraman spent her free time reading the newspaper and Fareed's books and having literary discussions with him.

"How many books did you write?"
"I have five books that are published and two books that are not published yet."
"Planning to publish these books anytime soon?"
"One will be published soon and the second I am working on the final draft."
"The play we saw together is your first?"
"It is my second play and it is giving me the exposure I need."
"Everybody needs exposure or else he or she is doing it for nothing."

"I have seen most of your movies but they were all romantic comedies except you're last movie 'The Dancer' which was a bit different. You never acted drama, why don't you try it?"
"The scripts that I get are usually all romantic comedies and you know that I am not an actress to go that deep in acting."
"You are a natural performer. Just take lessons in acting and you will be capable of acting drama movies."
"I wouldn't want to fail."
"You will never fail. I will be there to support you."
"Thank you Fareed for believing in my capabilities."

They have been going out for a year. There were rumors about their relationship but the couple kept denying it.

"Dada, I am planning a short tour."
"Why?"
"I need money to finance my upcoming projects."
"What do you have in mind?"
"It is a surprise."
"You have done more than enough my dear."
"I promise you, only two more."

Kahraman thought of Fareed in every second of her time. It has been a year since they met and he still did not propose. She began to feel worried. Her short tour was a success and returned to Cairo to receive unexpected sad news. Salma died in a heart attack. Kahraman was devastated. The club was closed for the next two months. Kahraman went to visit her almost every other day, putting flowers on her grave and tearfully spoke to her.

Kahraman purchased Salma's club, hired an interior designer to change the entire concept of the place that would hold her name. The dancer would dance only twice a week, precisely in the weekends and the rest of the evenings would be only a restaurant with an orchestra playing. She hired new management and advertised for its opening.

After her first performance in her own club, Kahraman thanked her guests for coming and declared that she would be performing only twice a week. The income of one of the two shows would go to the children she is taking care of then bid them good night. The dancer changed her clothes and met Fareed backstage.

"I did not expect your generosity would reach to this degree."
"I want my children to have everything."
"But they are young to know anything."
"I cannot resist that lost look in their tearful eyes."
"You have a heart of gold Kahraman, but make sure you keep something aside for your own children."

Kahraman felt her facial expressions betray her and quickly turned to the backstage door to leave as she was surprised by a group of photographers and journalists. Fareed held Kahraman tightly to him and guided her to the car. It was confirmed that the influential dancer and the reputable author were in a relationship. In the car, Fareed observed Kahraman who looked nervous. He kept remembering her facial expressions in the last seconds of his conversation with her which sparked a lot of questions. In his memory, he repeated their conversation which resulted finally with an answer to his question.
One evening, Kahraman was sitting in the living room studying her photos when Fareed arrived.
"Habebty, how are you this evening?"
Kahraman smiled and stood to greet him, "relaxing, how was your day?"
"My day was complex with lots of reading and writing."
"I like what I hear."
"I got you another book of mine to keep you company when I am not around."

Kahraman read the name and said, "I have all of your novels except this one. How did you know that I did not have it?"
"I figured it out, since you discussed all my novels with me except this one which happens to be the oldest and the most difficult to find."
Kahraman smiled brightly and said, "You haven't dedicated any of your books to me. I think its time, don't you think?"
"You are absolutely right which is what I did with this book."
"Since you are reading my thoughts, why don't you read your dedication to me?"
"On one condition, only if you admit that what I will read to you is also in your thoughts?"
Without hesitation Kahraman agreed. Fareed smiled gently and began reading what he wrote her:

'I saw in these eyes, warmth and tenderness that I never saw. I sensed in this soul, purity and loyalty that I never knew existed. I touched in this heart, compassion and trust that I never felt before. All these rare qualities are in a gem in the name of Kahraman, the lady that I want to spend the rest of my life with. Allow my thoughts to revolve around you, grant my pen to write words only for you, and let me say, I love you.'

Kahraman's eyes were glimmering with tears and hidden fears.
"Does your silence means you accept?" asked Fareed gently.
"Fareed, I have something to tell you that might make you withdraw your proposal."
"Tell me and I will decide for myself."
"I...I cannot conceive children."
With a tender look, Fareed said, "I know."
"How did you know?"
"I knew it on the night of the opening of your club. The topic of children seemed an obsession to you which inspired you to do these projects for them. When I questioned you regarding the topic of children, your reaction betrayed you. I never saw

you react in this manner which left a question in my thoughts. I analyzed the situation which resulted in this answer. I just needed a conformation from you."

"Since you know, why did you propose?"

"I proposed because my love for you exceeds you giving me children or not."

"Your parents must want to see your children and maybe in the future you'd yearn to have one."

"My parents are the ones who insisted that I don't delay proposing. I would never ask you to give me anything beyond your capabilities."

Kahraman's tears rained on her cheeks as Fareed kissed them away. He bent on his knee and said, "Marry me."

Kahraman bent on her knee and said, "Yes."

People were judging and criticizing Kahraman in a harsh manner. To some people she was known as one of the greatest artists of their time. To some people she was known as a clever business woman who knew how to make good money. To some people, she was simply a whore. The common people supported her while the rich people looked down at her. No matter how she was labeled, people still wanted to see her perform and eagerly followed her news. Kahraman disregarded the labels and concentrated on her art.

Kahraman was happy to wear a simple gold ring that Fareed gave her and secretly wed in the author's family house in the country with the presence of his parents and Hanan as the only attendants. The bride wore a simple white taffeta bridal gown for the first time. Misty eyes looked at newly weds as they ate the wedding cake. The couple flew to Paris for their short honeymoon before returning to a fully booked schedule. Kahraman's spokesperson released the news of her wedding to the reputable author and thinker Fareed Fahmi causing another stir all over the Middle East. The couple paid no attention to any remarks and focused on each other's love and support.

"I have been thinking of opening a small art university."
"You can't be serious Kahraman?"
"I am Fareed."
"Do you have enough money to make this project?"
"Yes, I can afford to make this project. My agent is preparing an international tour for me to have more money plunged into the project. My project's manager unexpectedly reported to me large sums of money from my dancing school, educational school and a recruitment office."
"Who will be managing it?"
"I will put a principle to manage it just like the school but you my dear will supervise the project completely."
"Me?"
"Yes, I know you are capable."
"But I am in the process of finalizing my book and doing my PHD."
"Should I beg Fareed?"
"Hayati, you will never need to beg me for anything. I will supervise the project if it makes you happy."
"That would make me tremendously happy."

Kahraman was busy preparing to embark on her first international tour that will have a mixture of Oriental, Western and Latin dances with expensive stage productions and lavish costumes. The tour begins in the USA then moving towards Europe and finally ending in the Middle East. Fareed would finish writing his novel and studies for his PHD.

After seeing her dance, people commented: 'She moves her arms like butterfly wings.' 'Her fluid like body moved like water.' 'She majestically mastered the art of dance.' 'She moved through the air with poise.'

"How can people smile when they know that there are children who are homeless and need help?"

☙

"Will the people respect and take me seriously now? Who cares anyway?"

☙

"I did not expect such a sacrifice from a man."

☙

"I will never let sadness creep into my life again."

☙

"I love challenges and I wait there arrival from time to time."

☙

Days passed, giving Kahraman more success and stardom. Fareed finished writing the ending of his much awaited novel and continued studying his PHD in philosophy. One evening, he received a call from Kamel, a friend first and a producer secondly inviting him to dinner. Fareed accepted the invitation that resulted in an agreement to a movie based on his novel to a film. Kamal took the risk and insisted on Kahraman being the lead actress though she has no drama acting experience. Fareed could not give him a reply till he discusses it with his wife who was coming this week from her international tour. The dancer returned anxiously to see her loved ones as she showered them with gifts, and stories. Kahraman was resting for the entire week when Fareed opened the topic of the movie.

"Habebe, you know I am not an actress in the first place, it was just a coincidence that made me one."
"Why don't you take private acting classes with a friend of mine who teaches acting in his own institute?"
"Will I have enough time?"
"Yes because I have to start writing the novel in script format and in that time you can start with the acting classes. It all depends how fast you grasp the acting techniques. Also, you have read the book and you know the type of character you are going to portray on screen. Begin practicing the scenes and eventually you will master them."

Fareed was able to convince his wife who started taking the classes with complete dedication yet still keeping an eye on her projects. The university is still in the process of assembly, making Kahraman excited to see the results. Her spokesperson released the news of Kahraman taking acting classes to act in her first drama movie based on the last bestseller novel of Fareed Fahmi. Some made sarcastic comments, some was worried if she is capable of doing so, some anxiously awaited and some believed she can do it. The dancer on the other side was secretly worried and nervous. She is to portray a mentally disturbed woman in an asylum which meant no costumes, dances, make-up and hair or romance with a handsome lead actor, just her and her acting to be seen. Fareed realized the tensions of his wife and kept reassuring her that she is capable of doing it.

The shooting began after months of practice and studying the script well. Producer Kamal expected to guide the dancer and there but was taken back as the rest of the casting crew with her profound acting in a touching manner as she portrayed the character. Fareed who was always on the set was proud of his wife's achievement and decided that she would act in all of his upcoming movies or plays based on his books.

Sitting between Fareed and Kamel, Kahraman watched the movie silently in the booth in the opening night for critics, VIP guests and the media. Surprised by a thunder of applause, the dancer's eyes were misty as her husband hugged her and people congratulated her.

The movie 'Chaos' was rated as 'the best movie she ever made' and 'a masterpiece' which gave Kahraman the confidence in doing more risky projects like acting in Fareed's upcoming play 'The Woman' live on stage in theatre. She was able to prove that she can act apart from dancing and that gave her freedom to be experimental in selecting movie roles in the future.

In the coming year, the art university was opened, making Kahraman the most talked about celebrity in the Middle East, specifically in Egypt. The couple bought gradually a small flat in the heart of Cairo, a small house in the country side and another small house facing the beach, furnishing it simply with an interior designer. Discussing and consulting each other in their respective work lead to cementing their professional relationship with trust, not forgetting the faith they had for one another and a pure love to last a test of time.

"Kahraman's waist can move nations."

-Jalal Rushdi, Al Fan Magazine

☙

"Her fusion of ballet and salsa with belly dancing created an entire new genre in dance."

-Raouf Ahmad, Al Ibdaa Magazine

☙

"Watching Kahraman dance made me reach to a stage of euphoria."

-Kamal Badri, Al Yom Newspaper

☙

"She took the art of belly dancing to international standards."

-Mamdooh Satar, Hyatt We Fan Magazine

☙

"The world would be at her feet in every performance."

-Zakaria Aleem, Fikr Newspaper

"When I look back at what I have achieved, I feel I have done nothing to stamp my name in history."

☙

"I find it a true joy to shock conventional people."

☙

"I'm growing older; almost reaching the age of maturity and that makes me feel fulfilled."

☙

"I feel I am highly enriched because life's experiences that has taught me countless vital matters that I will never learn from an educational institution."

☙

"Building a name as a trademark is no easy work. But once you make one, you will forget all that hardships you went through."

☙

"I will never feel ashamed of anything I have done in my life."

☙

"It is liberating to see people confused when they want to categorize or judge me, especially after what I did."

☙

"I have engraved my name in the souls of the people living in my time and for the coming generations."

☙

"I will always stand up high and unmovable like a mountain."

☙

"When they write something about Fareed, I want to be in the following page after him."

☙

"I thank God every night because I was given almost everything."

ଔ

"I'm very grateful to all the people who helped me."

ଔ

"I'm no longer that young, but I feel prettier than ever."

ଔ

"I was always aware of time, because it is limited. So I had to take advantage of it."

ଔ

"I feel blessed because I was able to work in what I wanted the most."

ଔ

Kahraman's artistic journey began in Oriental dance commonly known as belly dancing, adding Latin, African, Asian & Western dance to it. Yet, it was ballet that gave her the base to learn other dances apart from belly dancing. When she blended other dances with belly dancing, Kahraman became exceedingly creative in body movement to the exclusively composed music as well as in costumes and stage productions.

☙

"I heard of celebrities sufferings before reaching stardom. I don't believe I have suffered anything like them, thanks to my grandmother who made my life easy and for meeting the right people in the appropriate time. Let me say I am fortunate. I never had to degrade myself for anything. My achievements were the result of hard work. Yet, that is not always the case with celebrities."

☙

"Is it necessary to live a miserable life to become a legend? Unfortunately, most legendary people had tragic lives before they reached success and some still had it after they have reached success. One can lead a normal life, and become successful at the same time. What I am trying to say is that one should be a believer of her dreams, follow it with positive attitude and work hard to achieve it."

☙

"What kind of a woman am I? Persistent, especially when I know I am right. Creative and that is the core reason of my success. Hard worker, I believe you achieve nothing in life unless you are a hard worker. Generous, maybe because I had nothing then suddenly had everything. I wanted to share what I had with everyone. Dreamer, I did not enjoy living my reality when I was young so I became a dreamer."

www.ingramcontent.com/pod-product-compliance
Ingram Content Group UK Ltd.
Pitfield, Milton Keynes, MK11 3LW, UK
UKHW040019200726
13854UKWH00001B/269

9 781449 033101